About the Book

My name is Pat Logan. My brother's name is Brian. And Clarence is our dog.

Clarence is the friendliest dog I know. He never snarls or growls, even at strangers. He'd much rather play his favorite games, Fish and Ball, or, better still, watch TV. "Some watchdog!" says George Harris, next door.

But the night the burglar came, Clarence surprised us all....

That Clarence is quite a dog!

This delightfully funny story about Clarence has been adapted especially for beginning readers from Patricia Lauber's CLARENCE THE TV DOG, and illustrated by Paul Galdone with pictures as playful and bouncy as Clarence himself.

PAUL GALDONE
drew the pictures

Coward, McCann & Geoghegan, Inc. • New York

Weekly Reader Children's Book Club presents

clarence

and the

burglar

Adapted by F. N. Monjo
from a chapter in
Clarence the TV Dog
by PATRICIA LAUBER

My name is Pat Logan.

My brother's name is Brian.

And we have a dog

named Clarence.

Almost everybody on our street
loves Clarence because
he's so friendly.
He never growls at anybody.
He never growls at the Brundages.
He never growls at the Harrises.
He doesn't snarl at the mailman.
He doesn't snarl at the milkman.

He doesn't even snarl or growl
at strangers.

"Some watchdog!"
says George Harris.
George lives next door. He has
a great big dog named Wolf.

George and Wolf
make fun of Clarence
because Clarence never
growls at anybody.

"Hey, Mom," asks Brian,
"do you think there's
something wrong with Clarence?"
"No, Brian," says Mom.
"There's nothing wrong
with Clarence.
He's just friendly."
"Too friendly," says George.
"He'll never make a watchdog."
"I just wish he'd growl at *you!*"
Brian says.
But Clarence just wags his tail.
Well, Clarence may not be
much of a watchdog,
but he loves to play games.

The two he loves best

are called Fish

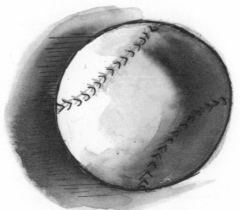

and Ball.

When Clarence plays Fish,
he runs and gets
his rubber fish.
He bites Fish until it squeaks.
Then he drops it at your feet.
And you're supposed to
hide Fish and let
Clarence find it.

When he plays Ball,
he drops his tennis ball
into your lap.
And you're supposed to throw it,
so Clarence can run after it
and fetch it back to you.
Clarence tries to get everybody
to play Fish or Ball with him.
If you don't want
to play games with him,
do you know what Clarence does?
He unties your shoelaces
with his teeth!
"Darndest dog I ever saw,"
says Brian,

and Clarence just wags his tail.

There's something else
that Clarence loves to do.
He loves to watch TV.
Every time our set is on,
Clarence watches with
Brian and me.

He likes to watch cartoons.

He likes cowboys and Indians.

He even likes commercials.

But he likes to watch
football games most of all.

Any Saturday
when Brian and his friends
are watching football,

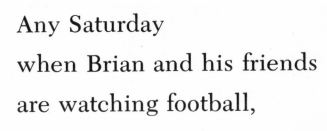

Clarence is there
in front of the TV,
watching with them.

So Mom puts an old bedspread
over a chair,
just for Clarence.
Now he knows that
that's his special chair.
And that's where he sits
when he's watching TV.

Sometimes, when
all of us are out,
Clarence goes next door
to visit Mr. and Mrs. Brundage.
If Clarence hears them
playing their TV,
he scratches on their door,
and they let him in.

Then Clarence sits down
in front of the TV
with Mr. and Mrs. Brundage
and watches football, too.

"He even barks when
State makes a touchdown!"
says Mr. Brundage.
(Mr. Brundage went to State.)
"Darndest dog I ever saw!"
And Clarence just wags his tail.

Now comes the part
about the burglar.
Because one Sunday night
Mom and Brian
and I went downtown
to the movies.
We left Clarence burying a bone
in the backyard.
There must have been
a night game on,
because Clarence went next door
to watch TV
with Mr. and Mrs. Brundage.

Then, while our house was
dark and empty,
a burglar opened a window
on the back porch.
He crept into our dining room.
And he began putting
Mom's table silver
into his sack.

Just then, the night game
must have ended on TV,
because Clarence came home
from the Brundages.
I guess he must have
scratched, first,
at the back door.
Then he came through
the window
the burglar left open.
Clarence hopped into
the dining room.
Inside he stopped and sniffed.
A stranger! Company!

A new friend!
Someone to play with!

When he saw the burglar,
he jumped up on him,
wagging his tail.
Then Clarence ran
to find Fish and Ball.
Clarence came back
first with Fish,
then with Ball.
He jumped up on the burglar
to say, "Let's play."
He nudged Ball with his nose.
He bit Fish until it squeaked.
But the burglar
was in a hurry,
and he didn't have time to play.

Clarence squeaked Fish again.
He dropped Ball
at the burglar's feet.

The burglar *still* didn't
want to play.
So Clarence reached down
and nipped first one shoelace,
and then the other,
until both the burglar's shoes
came untied.

And I guess that's
when we came home
from the movies.
Because as soon as we
walked into the house,
we heard a terrible crash
in the dining room.

We rushed in
and turned on the lights.

And there was the burglar
stretched out on the floor.
He was knocked out cold!

The sack of silver
was beside him.
And Clarence was
standing on the burglar's chest,
licking his face!

Brian got a baseball bat and
stood guard over the burglar.
Mom went to the telephone and
called the police.

Brian looked at Fish and Ball.

Then he looked at me and smiled.

"Clarence must have tried

to get him to play," I said.

"Then he untied

the burglar's shoes," said Brian.

"And the man tripped on his

shoelaces and fell," said Mom.

"And now he's out

like a light," said Brian.

Just then
George Harris
knocked on our front door.
Wolf was with him.
"Hey, someone just
robbed our house," said George.

"Wolf was asleep,
or he'd have caught him."
"Some watchdog," said Brian.
"The guy's right here, out cold
on our dining room floor.
Must be the same burglar.
He tried to rob our house, too.
Only our watchdog, Clarence,
was too smart for him.
Weren't you, Clarence?"
And Clarence just
wagged his tail.

Then we heard the sirens,
and the police came.
Sergeant Murphy put handcuffs
on the burglar.
"He sneaked in the porch window,"
said Sergeant Murphy, patting Wolf.

"And this big dog of yours
knocked him to the floor,
and the burglar was out
colder'n a mackerel."
"Not that big dog, Sergeant,"
said Brian.
"It's this *little* dog here.
It was *Clarence* who caught him!"

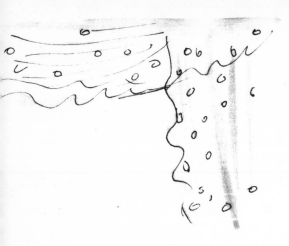
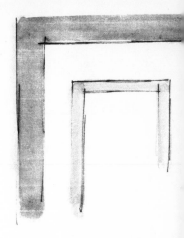

"Well, I'll be!"
said Sergeant Murphy.
"Some watchdog you got there!
He's a regular hero,
that Clarence!" And he
shook hands with Clarence.
And the Brundages came over
to find out what happened.
And so did George's Mom and Dad.

Sunny tracy,
high in 30s
Complete weather page 7a

The Jo

A MEMBER OF THE GANNETT GRO

The next day
Brian and Clarence and I
had our names in the paper.
And the headline said

PUP NABS BURGLAR

And there was a picture, too.
But Clarence's rear end
was only a blur

because he was wagging his
tail so hard.

About the Author

PATRICIA LAUBER has written more than forty books, but the first book she ever wrote is still her favorite. The title was *Clarence the TV Dog*, and it was all about her dog, Clarence, and his adventures. This story is taken from that first book, retold and adapted for younger readers.

Miss Lauber has written other stories about horses and dogs and also many highly successful nonfiction books.

When she is not writing, she likes to travel, sail, hike, cook, listen to music, and read. She lives in Connecticut, in a house that was once a barn.

About the Artist

PAUL GALDONE grew up in Budapest, Hungary, and came to the United States at the age of fourteen. He studied at the Art Students League in New York before beginning an extremely successful career as a children's book illustrator. He has illustrated more than 100 books, and has also written and adapted several books for which he did the illustrations. He has twice been runner-up for the Caldecott Award.

Paul Galdone lives in Rockland County, New York, and spends his summers in Tunbridge, Vermont, where he has a wonderful vegetable garden.